Brush
Two

Three

Tap
Four

Tallulah's Tap Shoes

by MARILYN SINGER

Illustrations by

ALEXANDRA BOIGER

CLARION BOOKS

Houghton Mifflin Harcourt | Boston | New York

Thanks to Steve Aronson, Yvonne Curry, Cara Gargano, and Laurie Shayler, and to my spectacular editor, Jennifer Greene, and all the good folks at Clarion.

Clarion Books
215 Park Avenue South, New York, New York 10003

Clarion Books is an imprint of Houghton Mifflin Harcourt Publishing Company.
www.hmhco.com

The text was set in Pastonchi MT Std.
The illustrations were executed in watercolor, as well as watercolor mixed with gouache and egg yolk, on Fabriano watercolor paper.

Library of Congress Cataloging-in-Publication Data
Singer, Marilyn.
Tallulah's tap shoes / Marilyn Singer, Alexandra Boiger.
pages cm
Summary: Tallulah loves the grace and elegance of ballet and can pirouette perfectly but at dance camp struggles to learn tap.
ISBN 978-0-544-23687-5 (hardcover)
[1. Ballet dancing—Fiction. 2. Tap dancing—Fiction.
3. Dance—Fiction. 4. Camps—Fiction. 5. Perseverance (Ethics)—Fiction.] I. Boiger, Alexandra, illustrator. II. Title.
PZ7.S6172Tajp 2015
[E]—dc23
2014021786

Manufactured in China
SCP 10 9 8 7 6 5 4 3 2 1
4500514800

To Tessa and her mother, Sarah
—M.S.

To all the little—and not so little—dancers
—A.B.

Tallulah was excited about going to dance camp.
She would get to take ballet every day.

There was just one problem—she would also have to take tap, and she was NOT looking forward to THAT. She'd been taking ballet for a while now and knew a lot of steps, but in tap, she'd be a *very beginning* beginner.

"I can't wait to take tap," said her little brother, Beckett.
"I want to dance *clickety-clack-clickety-clack.*" He shuffled his feet.
Tallulah sniffed. "I'm a ballet girl. I don't clickety-clack."

There were lots of ballet students at camp.

The beginners were in the front. The dancers who'd been studying a little longer were in the rear. The beginners pointed their feet in a tendu, then slid to the side in a glissade.

The teacher told Beckett that he didn't have to slide so much,
and she told a girl with shiny black hair to slide more.
I learned that last year, Tallulah thought.

Her group got to
practice a tombé

to a pas de bourrée

to a glissade.
She did it perfectly.

"That was lovely, Lulu!" said the teacher, a tiny, gray-haired woman with a nice smile.

"Thank you," Tallulah replied. She didn't bother to correct her. She figured she would know her name soon enough.

"Wasn't that great?" Tallulah said to the black-haired
girl as they changed clothes.

"*Great?* I don't think so," the girl replied. "I don't know
why we have to take ballet. It's so . . . stiff! Tap dancing
is so much cooler."

Tallulah's eyebrows shot up. "Stiff? Ballet is . . . elegant!"
She pirouetted gracefully around the floor.

But when she finished, the girl was gone.

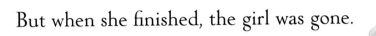

After ballet, Tallulah turned cartwheels in gymnastics,

went swimming in the lake,

ate a tuna sandwich for lunch,

and started to make a
friendship bracelet. All
of these things were fun—
but Tallulah was worried
about what was coming next.

"Time for tap!" shouted Beckett.

"Hurry up!"

Tallulah did not want to hurry up.

She dragged her feet on the way to the studio.

She took her time putting
on her brand-new tap shoes.

She was last to line up.

The teacher was a tall man with a deep voice. "We're going to start with toe taps."

Tallulah tapped her toes. **This is baby stuff,** she thought. Maybe tap wasn't going to be so hard after all.

But then she listened to the back row. Their taps sounded a lot different. Not like baby stuff at all.

"Good job, Kacie," Tallulah heard the teacher say. The girl with the shiny black hair was smiling proudly.

The teacher did not praise Tallulah. "Keep tapping, Tallulah," he told her. "And lift up your toe more."

Tallulah sighed. Why did *he* have to know her name?

When class ended, Tallulah had to wait for Beckett, who wouldn't stop tapping until the teacher made him. Kacie caught up with them.

"Now, THAT was a cool class," she said.

"*Cool? Clickety-clack-clack-clack!*" Tallulah answered back. "That's not dancing—it's just making noise."

"It's making MUSIC with your FEET!" Kacie told her.

"*Humph,*" said Tallulah.

Kacie humphed back.

Every day that week, Tallulah couldn't wait to go to ballet class. She was learning new steps and getting better at old ones. The teacher even asked her to demonstrate a rond de jambe.

And every day Tallulah dreaded going to tap class. She kept trying to get her feet to make music the way Kacie's did. But instead of praise, Tallulah got lots of corrections:

"Tallulah, make more of a sound."

"Tallulah, relax your ankles."

"Tallulah, don't point your toes."

When the teacher asked Kacie to do a *tap* rond de jambe,
Tallulah bit her lip and squeezed her eyes shut so she wouldn't cry.

In this class,
I'm not the
best student—
I'm the WORST.

Then one day, Kacie did not show up for ballet class.

When it came time for tap, Tallulah said to herself, **If she doesn't go to ballet, why should I go to tap?** She told her brother that she was going to stay in the arts-and-crafts room and finish her friendship bracelet.

"But Tallulah, you *never* miss dance class," Beckett said.

"I never miss *ballet* class," Tallulah replied.

"But don't you want to learn other things besides?" Beckett asked.

Tallulah lowered her eyes and shrugged.

When Tallulah got home, her mother said they
were having guests for dinner—some people she and
Tallulah's father met at a party. "Their daughter goes
to dance camp, too."

Tallulah was not in the mood to see anyone from dance camp.
She was not in the mood for any company at all.

She went to her room and stared in the mirror.

She did an arabesque
she'd learned in ballet.
It was beautiful.

Then she put on her tap shoes
and tried a flap step.
It was not beautiful at all.

I'm a ballet girl, she reminded herself.
So what if I can't be a tap dancer, too?

But that thought didn't make her feel better.

She slumped on her bed, her head in her hands.
Then Beckett opened the door. "Tallulah, we've got
company! Look who's here!"

Tallulah turned around. Kacie was standing there, frowning and twisting the friendship bracelet on her wrist.

"You!" Tallulah exclaimed, jumping to her feet. "Where were you in ballet today?"

"Me? Where were *you* in tap?"

"I *hate* tap!" Tallulah shouted.

"I hate *ballet!*" Kacie cried.

Beckett looked
from one upset face
to the other.
"Why?" he asked.

Both girls turned to him and blinked.

Tallulah fiddled with her friendship bracelet. Finally, she asked curiously, "Why *do* you hate ballet?"

Kacie took a while to answer. "I don't really hate ballet," she admitted at last. "It's just . . . in tap class, I'm the best. But in ballet, I'm the worst."

"You're not the worst." Tallulah was surprised. "Not at all."

"But the teacher's always correcting me!"

"Teachers *always* correct *everybody*," Tallulah said.

Then her eyes opened wide. "They always correct everybody," she repeated, more softly.

"Well, you aren't the worst in tap," Kacie told her. "If you keep practicing, you'll get better. Then you might love it. And maybe we could even take classes together."

"And you might love ballet," Tallulah said. Then, with a little smile, she added, "And take classes with me."

"I love tap *and* ballet already," Beckett said, which made both girls laugh.

The next day, in ballet,
Kacie slipped doing her glissade,
but she still wasn't the worst in class.

And in tap, Tallulah's flap steps sounded
louder and clearer, but she still wasn't the best.
Maybe I'm right where **I'm supposed
to be,** Tallulah thought. **For now.**

And that was what she told Kacie that very afternoon as they waited, wearing each other's friendship bracelets, with Beckett flapping and glissading happily between them, until the bus came to take them all home.

Flap Step

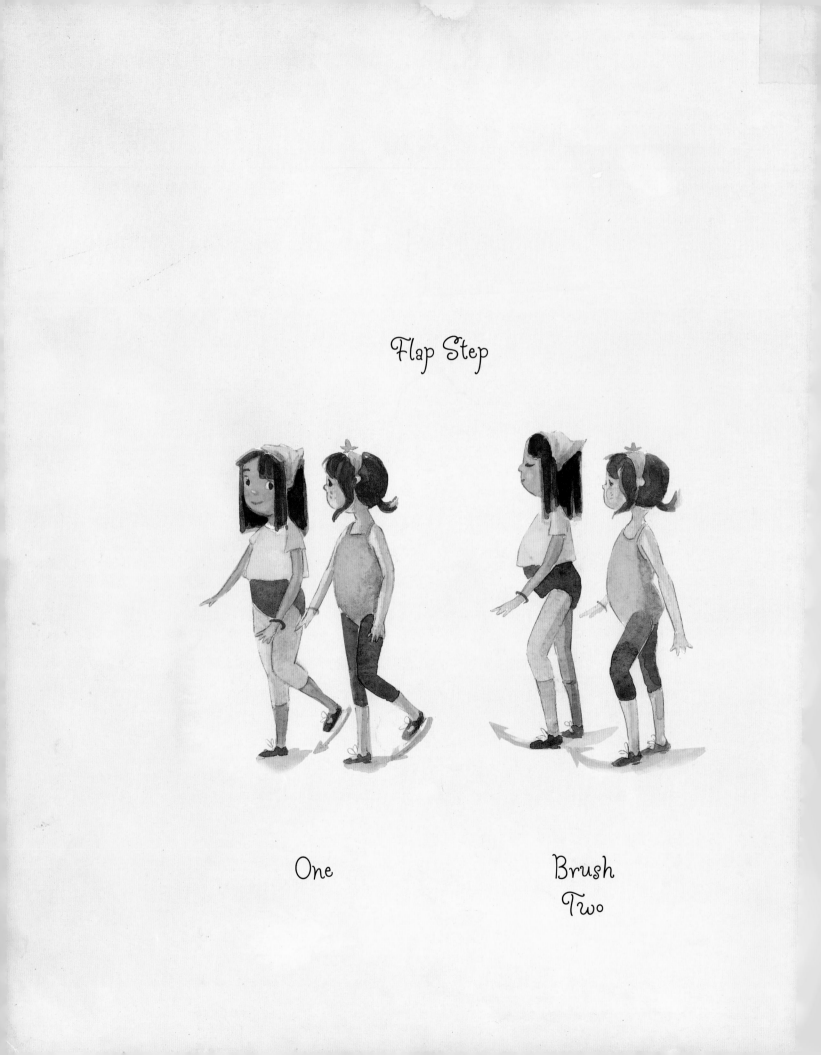

One

Brush
Two